W9-BZO-581

FAIRY TALES

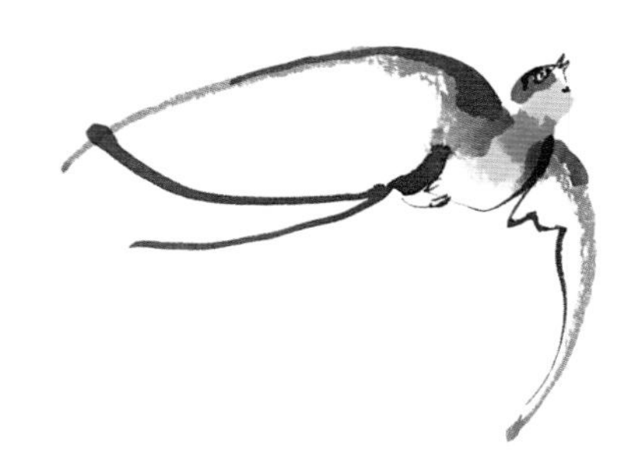

Also by E. E. Cummings

The Enormous Room

Tulips & Chimneys

is 5

ViVa

No Thanks

22 and 50 Poems

1 x 1 [One Times One]

XAIPE

95 Poems

73 Poems

Etcetera

Complete Poems 1904–1962

Selected Poems

FAIRY TALES

E. E. Cummings

Edited, with an Afterword, by George James Firmage

Illustrated by Meilo So

LIVERIGHT
NEW YORK LONDON

Printed in China

For information about permission to reproduce selections from this book, write to Permissions, W. W. Norton & Company, Inc., 500 Fifth Avenue, New York, NY 10110

Manufacturing by RR Donnelley, Shenzhen
Book design by Chris Welch
Production manager: Andrew Marasia/Julia Druskin

Library of Congress Cataloging-in-Publication Data

Cummings, E. E. (Edward Estlin), 1894–1962.

Fairy tales / E. E. Cummings; edited, with an afterword, by
George James Firmage;
illustrated by Meilo So.
p. cm.
Summary: Four tales include "The Old Man Who Said 'Why'," "The Elephant and The Butterfly," "The House That Ate Mosquito Pie," and "The Little Girl Named I."
ISBN 0-87140-658-6
1. Fairy tales—United States. [1. Fairy tales.] I. Firmage, George James.
II. So, Meilo ill. III. Title.

PZ8.C9Fai 2004
[E]—dc22

2003070238

Liveright Publishing Corporation
500 Fifth Avenue, New York, N.Y. 10110
www.wwnorton.com

W. W. Norton & Company Ltd.
15 Carlisle Street, London W1D 3BS

2 3 4 5 6 7 8 9 0

CONTENTS

The Old Man Who Said "Why"

Once there was a faerie who lived on a farthest star. He was very good-natured and had yellow hair and blue eyes. Everybody in the air and everywhere and in all the stars respected him, and took all their troubles to him whenever something went wrong. For millions of years he lived quietly and happily without growing any older (because he was a faerie and faeries never grow any older) and he was very polite and he had a wonderful smile and a pair of golden wings.

All the people on the stars and everywhere and in the air had wings too (although they weren't faeries themselves) because to travel in the air and everywhere from one star to another star you have to fly. In fact, the people were flying most of the time. They would open their wings and fly down to breakfast, and then fold up their wings and eat breakfast. When it was lunch time, they would fly from the air, or wherever they were playing, into their houses; and fold up their wings and have a delicious luncheon made of star-petals and air-flowers. Then they'd fly upstairs and have a little nap, and when they woke up they'd fly out the window to play again away up in the air. And after supper they'd fly to bed and fall fast asleep, to dream all night about rainbows.

It wasn't very often that these people had troubles to take to the faerie; but whenever they had them, they'd fly over to the farthest star where he lived, taking their troubles with them under their arms; and he would examine all the troubles (no matter how big or how little they were, or

whether they were just plain troubles or troubles in fancy boxes tied up with pink and green ribbons) and he'd give advice to all the people who brought him these troubles and would never charge them even ten cents. He liked to be nice to people, you see.

Well, after this faerie had lived happily and quietly for millions and millions of years, he woke up one morning on the farthest star and heard a murmuring all around him in the air, and this murmuring seemed to come from all the other stars. "Why what in the sky is happening?" he said to himself. All the while he was eating his breakfast, this murmuring kept getting louder and louder and louder and louder and louder and louder and louder—till finally the faerie hopped up from the table with a plate of light in one hand and a glass of silence in the other (for he always breakfasted upon light and silence) and cried: "My gracious! Whatever is going on over there on the other stars!" He was so nervous he spilled the silence and choked on the light and then went running out very quickly on the porch. There he saw a strange sight: all the air and everywhere around his star was growing dark, and as he looked, it got darker and darker and darker and darker and darker and darker—until finally the faerie struck a match because he couldn't see. Then this darkness turned into people: he saw that the air and everywhere was dark because it was filled with millions and millions and millions and millions and millions of people. "Good Heavens!" exclaimed the faerie—"what *can* be the matter? Are all these people coming to see me and bringing their troubles? What *shall* I do?"

He was really quite scared; but he wouldn't admit it; so he lit a candle and put on his hat and looked very wise. In a few moments the star on which he lived began to be filled with millions and millions and millions and millions of winged people who'd alighted on it. Millions and millions and millions of people began hopping and flopping and tripping and skipping and scurrying and tumbling and grumbling and hurrying toward his house. They came so fast they almost blew out his candle: in a few seconds he found himself surrounded by millions and millions of angry neighbors, all of them carrying troubles—and the funny

part of it was these troubles all looked alike; so he knew that all the people must have the same trouble.

Before the faerie could say as much as "hello" or "how do you do" or "are you well" or "what's the matter," the millions of troubled angry people cried out together in chorus: "We want you to help us all quickly and if you don't we'll all go mad!"

The faerie took off his hat quickly and held it before the candle—which had almost gone out because the people shouted so loudly. "But what in the air is the matter?" he cried to the millions and millions and millions and millions and millions and millions and millions and millions of angry people.

And in one voice they all answered together: "It's the man who says 'why'!"

"Where is he?" the faerie cried, very much surprised.

"On the moon!" they all shouted, waving their troubles very fiercely.

"Well, what do you wish me to do about him?" the faerie said wisely, although he was so surprised that he didn't have a single thought in his blond head.

"You must stop him from saying 'why'!" the people screamed all together.

"Of course, of course," the faerie promised. "Just you all go home and everything will be all right by, let me see—tomorrow morning."

"Where shall we leave our troubles?" they bellowed.

"Please to put them in the garden, under the third apple tree," the faerie said; and all the people rushed to the faerie's little garden and laid their troubles under the third apple tree which was a thousand miles tall and had red and green apples on it as big as balloons; and by the time that the last person had left his trouble, there was a pyramid of troubles around the tree right up to the apples. Then all the people politely thanked the faerie (for they were very much relieved) and they dusted their clothes and straightened their neckties and all flew away.

When they had all flown away, and the farthest star was perfectly quiet again, the faerie went into his house and looked in a large book which his mother had given him, and which told him what to do. He looked under "trouble" and under "man" and under "the" and "moon" and "why,"

but couldn't find a single bit of advice. "Well I never," exclaimed this faerie. "I guess I'll have to do it all by myself!"

So, after scratching his head for five minutes, he sighed and opened his golden wings and flew out into the air and everywhere, in the direction of the moon.

He flew all night and he flew millions and millions and millions of miles; and at last (just toward morning) he saw the moon away off, looking no bigger than a penny; but as he flew toward it, it got bigger and bigger and bigger until he could see it clearly; and finally, flying very hard, he came to the very edge of the moon. And then he saw a high rock, right on the very edge of the moon, and on top of this rock there was a tall church, and on the top of this church there was a slender steeple, and away up—right at the very top of this steeple—there was sitting a very very very very very very very old man with little green eyes and a big white beard and delicate hands like a doll's hands. And this little old man never moved and sat all by himself looking and looking and looking at nothing.

The faerie stopped flying and alighted on the moon. He

folded his wings and walked up to the high rock and called to the little man, but the little man paid no attention. "That little man must be deaf," the faerie said to himself; and so he opened his wings again and flew up to the top of the rock and shouted: "Hello!" But the old old old man sitting on the steeple didn't move. "That's certainly a queer little old man," said the faerie. And so he opened his wings for the second time and flew up to the top of the church; and, standing on the roof, he cried out as loudly as ever he could to the very little old man on the steeple: "Come down!" But there was no answer and the little old man with the green eyes and the doll's hands didn't stir. "Well, I'll be wafted!" said the faerie in disgust, and so he opened his wings and flew quickly right up to the very top of the slender steeple, and alighted on it just beside the little old man; and bellowed with all his might: "What are you doing up here anyway?"

And the little very very very very very very very old man smiled, and looking at the faerie he said: "Why?"

"Because I've come all the way from the farthest star to see you," the faerie said.

"Why?" said the very very very very very very little old man.

"Just a moment and I'll tell you why," said the faerie. "I've heard a great many complaints about you—"

"Why?" said the little very very very very very old man.

"Because I've got ears, I suppose," the faerie said angrily. "Everybody in the air and everywhere and on all the stars is complaining about you and making a dreadful fuss."

"Why?" said the very very very very little old man.

"Because you say *why* all the time," said the faerie. "And it's driving everybody mad. People can't sleep and can't eat and can't think and can't fly because you're always saying why and why and why and why over and over and over again. And I've come from the farthest star to tell you that you've got to stop this why-ing."

"Why?" said the little very very very old man.

At this, the faerie grew pink with anger. "If you don't stop saying why," he said, "you'll be sorry."

"Why?" said the very very little old man.

"Now see here," the faerie said. "That's the last time I'll

forgive you. Listen to me: if you say why again, you'll fall from the moon all the way to the earth."

And the little very old man smiled; and looking at the faerie, he said "why?" and he fell millions and millions and millions of deep cool new beautiful miles (and with every part of a mile he became a little younger; first he became a not very old man and next a middle-aged man and then a young man and a boy and finally a child) until, just as he gently touched the earth, he was about to be born.

The Elephant & The Butterfly

Once upon a time there was an elephant who did nothing all day.

He lived by himself in a little house away at the very top of a curling road.

From the elephant's house this curling road went twisting away down and down until it found itself in a green valley where there was another little house, in which a butterfly lived.

One day the elephant was sitting in his little house and looking out of his window doing nothing (and feeling very happy because that was what he liked most to do) when along this curling road he saw somebody coming up and up toward his little house; and he opened his eyes wide, and felt very much surprised. "Whoever is that person who's coming up along and along the curling road toward my little house?" the elephant said to himself.

And pretty soon he saw that it was a butterfly who was fluttering along the curling road ever so happily; and the elephant said: "My goodness, I wonder if he's coming to call on me?" As the butterfly came nearer and nearer, the elephant felt more and more excited inside of himself. Up the steps of the little house came the butterfly and he knocked very gently on the door with his wing. "Is anyone inside?" he asked.

The elephant was ever so pleased, but he waited.

Then the butterfly knocked again with his wing, a little louder but still very gently, and said: "Does anyone live here, please?"

Still the elephant never said anything because he was too happy to speak.

A third time the butterfly knocked, this time quite loudly, and asked: "Is anyone at home?" And this time the elephant said in a trembling voice: "I am." The butterfly peeped in at the door and said: "Who are you, that live in this little house?" And the elephant peeped out at him and answered: "I'm the elephant who does nothing all day." "Oh," said the butterfly, "and may I come in?" "Please do," the elephant said with a smile, because he was very happy. So the butterfly just pushed the little door open with his wing and came in.

Once upon a time there were seven trees which lived beside the curling road. And when the butterfly pushed the door with his wing and came into the elephant's little house, one of the trees said to one of the trees: "I think it's going to rain soon."

"The curling road will be all wet and will smell beautifully," said another tree to another tree.

Then a different tree said to a different tree: "How lucky

for the butterfly that he's safely inside the elephant's little house, because he won't mind the rain."

But the littlest tree said: "I feel the rain already," and sure enough, while the butterfly and the elephant were talking in the elephant's little house away at the top of the curling road, the rain simply began falling gently everywhere; and the butterfly and the elephant looked out of the window together and they felt ever so safe and glad, while the curling road became all wet and began to smell beautifully just as the third tree had said.

Pretty soon it stopped raining and the elephant put his arm very gently around the little butterfly and said: "Do you love me a little?"

And the butterfly smiled and said: "No, I love you very much."

Then the elephant said: "I'm so happy, I think we ought to go for a walk together you and I: for now the rain has stopped and the curling road smells beautifully."

The butterfly said: "Yes, but where shall you and I go?"

"Let's go away down and down the curling road where I've never been," the elephant said to the little butterfly.

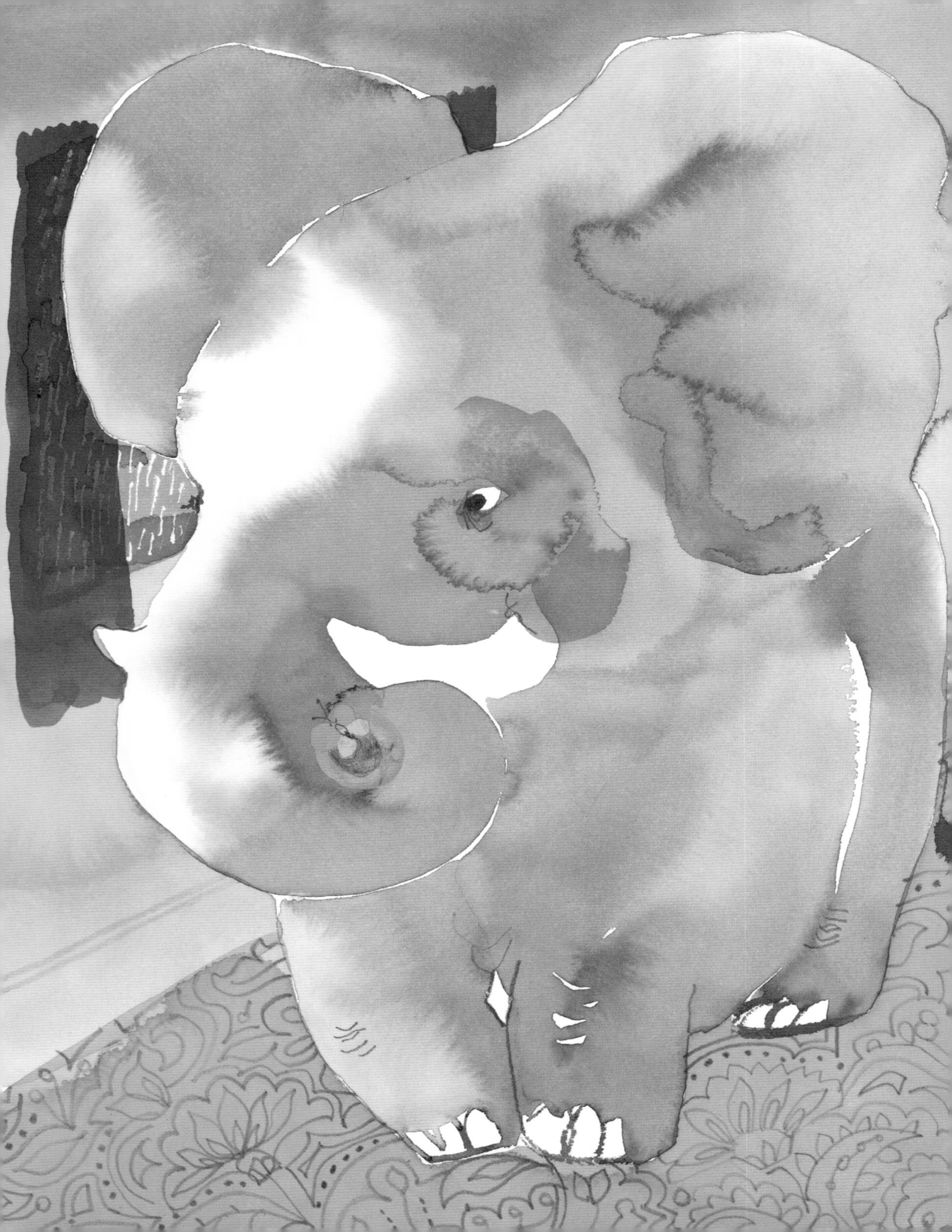

And the butterfly smiled and said: “I’d love to go with you away and away down the curling road—let’s go out the little door of your house and down the steps together—shall we?”

So they came out together and the elephant’s arm was very gently around the butterfly. Then the littlest tree said: “I believe the butterfly loves the elephant as much as the elephant loves the butterfly, and that makes me very happy, for they’ll love each other always.”

Down and down the curling road walked the elephant and the butterfly.

The sun was shining beautifully after the rain.

The curling road smelled beautifully of flowers.

A bird began to sing in a bush, and all the clouds went away out of the sky and it was Spring everywhere.

When they came to the butterfly’s house, which was down in the green valley which had never been so green, the elephant said: “Is this where you live?”

And the butterfly said: “Yes, this is where I live.”

“May I come into you house?” said the elephant.

“Yes,” said the butterfly. So the elephant just pushed the

2

door gently with his trunk and they came into the butterfly's house. And then the elephant kissed the butterfly very gently and the butterfly said: "Why didn't you ever before come down into the valley where I live?" and the elephant answered, "Because I did nothing all day. But now that I know where you live, I'm coming down the curling road to see you every day, if I may—and may I come?" Then the butterfly kissed the elephant and said: "I love you, so please do."

And every day after this the elephant would come down the curling road which smelled so beautifully (past the seven trees and the bird singing in the bush) to visit his little friend the butterfly.

And they loved each other always.

The House That Ate Mosquito Pie

Once there was a house who fell in love with a bird.

This house was tall and empty and had a great many windows. Nobody lived in him because he stood on top of a high hill, away off from anywhere, with no one except the morning to play with and no one except the sunset to talk with and no one except the twilight to confide in. There was the afternoon, of course; but the afternoon rarely came near the house because the afternoon was too busy putting the moon to bed. And there was the night, too; but the night was fondest of wandering and wandering among all the bright and gentle kinds of flowers which you and I call "stars" because we don't know what they really may be. So, except for the three friends—the morning, the sunset, and the twilight—this tall and empty house with a great many windows, standing on the top of a high hill, was all alone.

Now, one day, while the empty house was playing at shadows with the morning, and trying to amuse himself and forget how really lonely he was (away on top of the high hill) there was a sound in the air as if two or three or perhaps four white clouds were whispering together; and this sound came nearer and nearer the house, until the house knew that it was the wings of somebody who was flying and flying and flying. In a little while the house heard a new sound, which was as if five or six (or maybe seven) brooks were laughing about a secret; and this sound grew higher

and clearer until the house knew that it was somebody singing and singing and singing.

The house trembled all over with happiness and listened with all his might; and looked everywhere, out of all his windows, trying to see who the flying and singing somebody might be. Suddenly, out of the corner of one of his highest windows, he spied a little person floating and floating and floating in the air, and wiggling a pair of tiny wings, and singing as beautifully as if there were thousands of people to hear her song. This little person was all alone high up in the air over the green world, but her song tumbled gently down through the clouds and wandered everywhere along the green world, making it greener; and as it wandered along the world, this song seemed to be always looking for something or someone. At last the song came wandering (very gently) to the hill on which the house stood; and then the song paused, very gently, and seemed to find someone or something. After a moment, it began again and climbed slowly and gently up the hill; while the little person floated gently and slowly down and down and

down through the air; and the heart of the empty tall house stood quite still as the song and the flying person came nearer and nearer and nearer and nearer—for the house knew (all inside of himself) that the song was looking for nobody but him and that the singing floating flying person was coming to see him and nobody else, out of all the sunlight and all the air and all the world and all the sky.

And that was true.

Nobody can suppose how happy the house was when all at once the tiny flying person alighted right beside him and said: "May I come to live in you?" The house answered, very humbly and very happily: "Now I know why I have been very lonely for ever and ever such a long time—it was all for this day. Please live in me, and never stop living in me until we both stop living."

Then the bird thanked him and promised; and the house made all his rooms beautiful just by feeling happy and the bird wandered and wandered through all these beautiful rooms until she became so tired that she just went right to sleep in the queerest quietest tiniest tiptop room.

When the bird woke up the next morning, she found the house all filled with sunlight, and knew that she was happier than she had ever been before. So she sang to the house; and as for the house, he loved her so much he washed all his windows and wound up all his clocks and swept all his stairs and finally painted himself all over with fresh bright new paint—and by that time it was toward noon, and he felt hungry and tired.

"What shall we have for lunch?" he said to the bird.

The bird thought and thought. Finally she said: "Since you're such a beautiful house and since I love you so much, I should like to fly out and catch some mosquitoes so that we can have a bit of mosquito pie!"

"That's a fine idea," the house said, "for I'm really very hungry indeed, after painting myself all over new."

"I'll be right back," said the bird; and she flew out of a window in the house and went up up up up unto the sweet warm air, singing and singing and singing and singing, while the house looked after her, smiling all happily to himself and thinking: "My, how lucky a house I am after all!" But just when he thought she had disappeared (because he couldn't hear her singing any more) she came hurrying through the air silently down and down and down and very gently alighted in the tiptop window and whispered: "Sh! some people are coming!"

"People?" said the house; and he looked out. "I don't see any."

"They are coming up the hill," the bird whispered. "Don't you see them?" And as she spoke, it grew dark.

The house looked again—and sure enough, he saw three people climbing the hill. "By Jove!" he whispered, "what shall we do?"

"Let's keep very still," the bird whispered; and the house whispered: "All right," and the two of them cuddled close to one another and smiled to one another and didn't say anything, in the darkness.

Then up the road that led to the house came the three people and they all lifted their heads and said: "Ho! Look what's here! It's a house to be sure!" (and the house never said anything and the bird kept very still). Then up the hill to the door of the house came the three people and they all cried: "Ho! What's this? A tall house and an empty house and a full-of-windows house without anybody living in it!" (and the bird scarcely breathed and the house never said a word). Then up the steps and through the door and into the house came the three people and they all shouted: "Ho! We own this house, we do! And let anybody tell us differently!"—But just at this moment, what should happen but all the clocks in the house began striking and with such a banging and a crashing as you never heard and the people all jumped right up in the air with fright and ran around and around and out of the door and down the hill as fast as they could go; with the house laughing and laughing, and the bird fluttering and singing, and a great deal of sunlight quickly rushing all over the green world.

So then the bird flew out and caught mosquitoes until she had enough for a delicious pie; and she brought them

all back, and gave them to the house, who cooked them with a good deal of sugar and made them into a pie; and so the bird and the house each ate three big helpings of perfectly delicious mosquito pie (and let me tell you that they felt very well indeed afterwards).

Not only that—but no people ever bothered them any more, and so they were as happy together as happy could be.

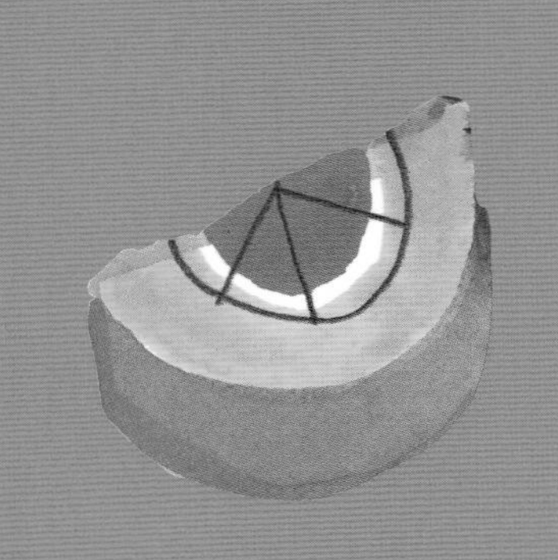

The Little Girl Named I

Once upon a time there was a little girl named I. She was a very good little girl, wasn't she? Yes indeed; very good. So one day this little girl named I was walking all by herself in a green green field. And who do you suppose she meets?

A cow, I suppose.

Yes, that's right. It was a yellow cow. So ever so politely

MADE IN CHINA

she says to this cow "How do you do" and what does this cow say?

Does it say "Nicely, thank you very much"?

Yes. It does. And so this little girl named I is very glad, and she invites this cow to come to tea, but this cow doesn't like tea. So then they say "Goodbye" and away goes I through the green green field, all by herself.

By

and by I was walking along and I saw a white horse eating green green grass. And what do you suppose this horse said?

Did he say "Hello"?

Yes, he did. And so this little girl named I said "Hello" too, just like that. And then they both laughed and laughed and when they got through laughing this little girl named I said to this white horse "I'm going to have tea and would you like to come along?" but this white horse didn't think he did.

You mean he didn't like tea?

Yes, that's right. And so then they said "Goodbye" and

away goes I through the green green field, all by herself.

By and by I was walking and walking when whoever do you suppose I should find, sleeping in the sun and fast asleep?

Was it a pig perhaps?

Yes. It was. A pink pig. And what did this little girl named I say?

I suppose she said "How do you do."

No. She didn't.

Did she say "Hello?"

No. She didn't say "Hello."

Well then what did she say?

She said "Good morning Mister Pig, and are you asleep?" And do you know what this pig said?

I guess he said he was.

No. He didn't.

Then I guess he said he wasn't.

No. He didn't say that either.

What did this pig say?

Well, he didn't say anything, because he was asleep. So

then I went tiptoeing away so as not to disturb him because he was asleep and ever so softly away goes I through the green green field all by herself.

Pretty soon

this little girl named I saw a tree.

What kind of a tree?

It was a pretty big tree.

Was it?

It was. And who do you suppose was under this pretty big tree, all by himself?

I don't know. You tell me.

Shall I?

Yes. Was it a duck?

No.

Well what was it then?

Why, it was an elephant.

Really?

Yes. It was.

Well now. And whatever was this elephant doing under the tree?

He was eating. He was.

Eating? What was he eating?

He was eating bananas, all by himself.

Oh, you mean these bananas grew away up on the tree?

Yes. They did. And he was pulling them down with his trunk and putting them into his mouth and eating them. He was.

Well well. What did the little girl named I say when she saw him do that?

When she saw him eating bananas, you mean?

Yes.

She said "It's a pleasant day, isn't it?" that's what she said to him. And he said to her "These bananas are delicious, will you have one?"

That was very nice of him, I think, to ask her if she'd like a banana.

I think it was nice, too. So then this little girl said "Thank you very much" she said "But I'm going to have some tea, myself."

Did she ask this elephant if he'd like to come to tea?

She did.

And what did he say?

This elephant, he said "Yes, I'd like to come to tea very much" he said.

Then he came to tea?

No. He didn't.

How was that? I thought he said he'd like to come.

He did. But then he said "I think I'd better eat these bananas that are growing up here, because if I should stop, they'd grow faster than I can eat them."

That was a very good answer.

Yes. It was. So this little girl named I said to this elephant "Are you joking with me, shame on you?" and he said "Yes, I am joking with you, shame on me." So then she made kewpie eyes for him and he made kewpie eyes for her and then away goes I through the green green field, all by herself.

Who did she meet then?

Well, she didn't meet anybody for a long long time. But after a while this little girl named I sees another little girl just like her.

You mean this other little girl looked just like this little girl named I?

Just just just like her.

That was funny, wasn't it?

Yes, it was. And I said to this other little girl "What's your name?" I said "Because I'd like to know" and this other little girl she never said anything.

Not anything?

No. And then I said to this other little girl, just like this I said "Who are you?"

And what did this other little girl say?

"You. That's who I am" she said "And You is my name because I'm You."

I suppose this little girl named I was surprised?

I was ever so surprised.

And what happened then?

Then I said to You "Would you like to have some tea?" I said. And You said "Yes. I would" You said. So then You and I, we went to my house together to have some tea and then we had some fine hot tea I suppose and some delicious bread and butter too, with lots and lots and lots of jam.

And that's the end of this story.

Afterword

BY GEORGE JAMES FIRMAGE

When *Fairy Tales* was first published in 1965, the author's widow, Marion Morehouse Cummings, prefaced the volume with the following note: "These tales were written for Cummings' daughter Nancy, when she was a very little girl." The statement is undoubtedly true for three of the tales—"The Old Man Who Said 'Why,' " "The House That Ate Mosquito Pie," and "The Little Girl Named I"—which were written sometime before Nancy's mother divorced Cummings in 1924 to marry an Irish businessman the following year and reside in Dublin. Despite an agreement that granted Cummings visiting rights, her mother's husband intervened and succeeded in not only keeping Nancy and her father apart but concealing from her the fact that Cummings was her father.

In 1940, Nancy, then a young lady of twenty, came to the United States, worked as a translator in Washington, D.C., met and married Willard Roosevelt, the grandson of President Theodore Roosevelt, in 1943, and gave birth to a son the following year. News that he was a grandfather reached Cummings through friends and apparently inspired him, in part, to write the play *Santa Claus*.

Nancy and her father finally met in 1946, but it wasn't until 1948, when he was painting her portrait in his New York studio, that Cummings actually told her he was her father. This event was significant for many reasons, not least of which was the writing of "The Elephant & The Butterfly." Richard Kennedy, the author of *Dreams in the Mirror: A Biography of E. E. Cummings*, has uncovered evidence that this tale was written sometime after 1948, and therefore not for "Nancy, when she was a very little girl." If I am not mistaken, the elephant, Cummings' "totem," represents the author, and the butterfly, another "he," is his grandson.